Jimmy's Boa Bounces Back

Farm Fresh PIGS

Each pig personally selected by master chef Monsieur ☆Butch☆

Boa Bounces Back

TRINKA HAKES NOBLE

pictures by STEVEN KELLOGG

PUFFIN BOOKS

For Eva C., Erica, and Jessica
T. H. N.

For Lucy the Great
S. K.

Dial Books for Young Readers
375 Hudson Street
New York, New York 10014

Text Copyright © 1984 by Trinka Hakes Noble
Pictures copyright © 1984 by Steven Kellogg
All rights reserved.
Library of Congress Catalog Card Number: 83-14289
Printed in the U.S.A.
First Pied Piper Printing 1987
COBE
20   19   18   17   16   15   14

A Pied Piper book is a registered trademark of
Dial Books for Young Readers, a division of Penguin Books USA Inc.
® TM 1,163,686 and ® TM 1,054,312.

JIMMY'S BOA BOUNCES BACK
is published in a hardcover edition by
Dial Books for Young Readers.
ISBN 0-14-054654-5

The full-color artwork was prepared using ink and pencil line
and watercolor washes. It was then color-separated and reproduced
as red, blue, yellow, and black halftones.

"Hi, Meggie. Where have you been all afternoon?"

"Oh, I had to serve cookies at my mom's garden club meeting, and you'll never guess who was there."

"Who?"
"Your boa."

"My boa!"

"Yeah, he must have run away from the farm."

"But how did he get to your mom's garden club?"

"Well, actually, my mom wore him."

"She wore him?"

"Yeah, she thought he would spruce up her old gray suit.
  All the garden club ladies thought she looked terrific."

"Wow, my mom wouldn't even touch him!"
"Well…you see…your boa had spent a cold night in the tree outside my house. So I told my mom that snakes don't move around much when they're cold and tired."

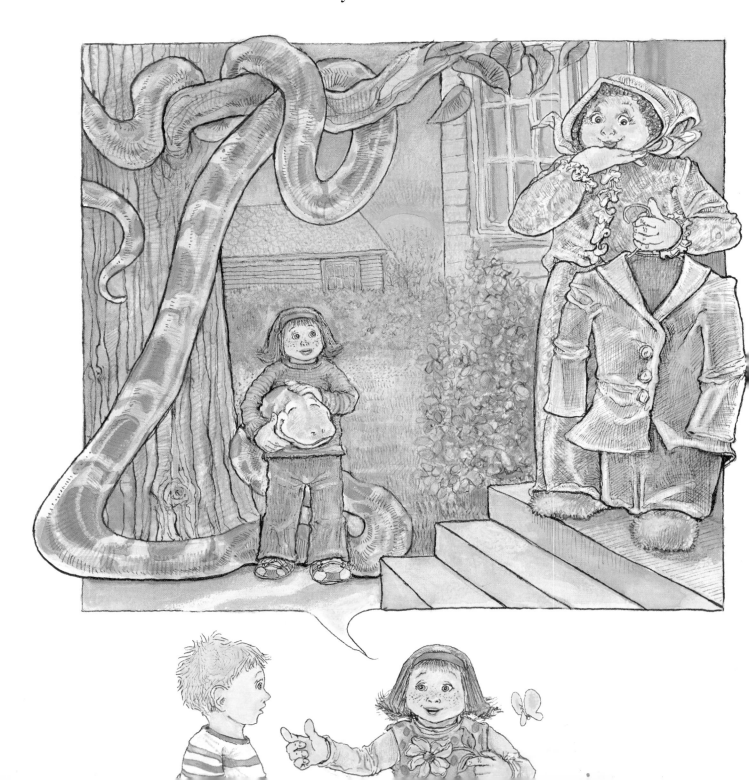

"Did he stay still?"

"He might have…except Mrs. Rosebud's wig flew off."

"She had on a flying wig!"

"Actually, it got caught on an alligator's tooth."

"You mean there were alligators at your mom's garden club?"

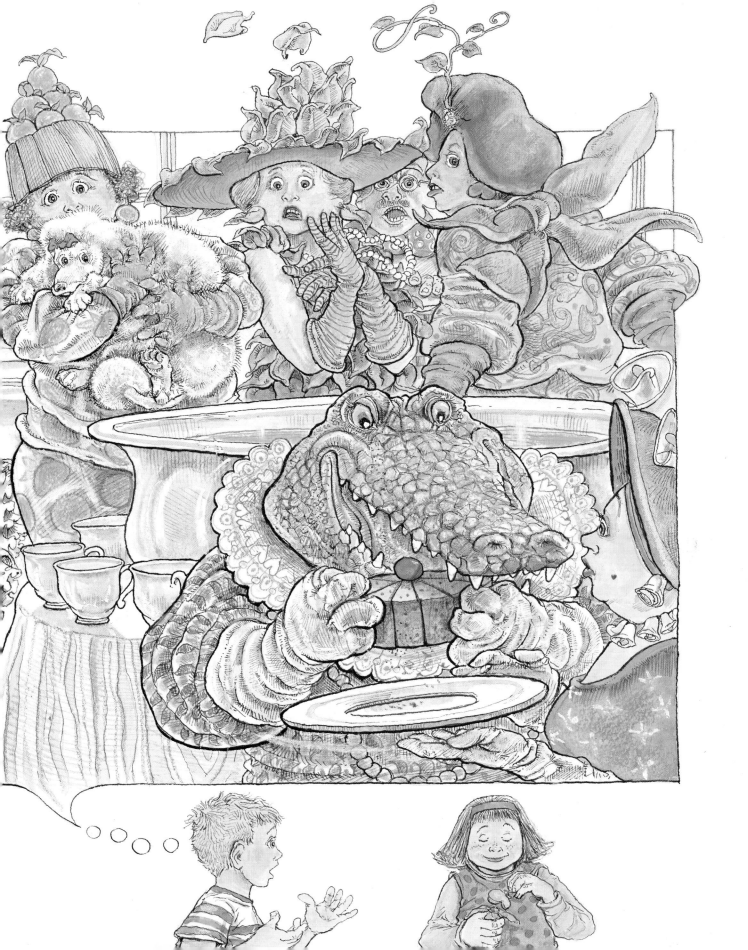

"Just one. It was Miss Greenleaf's alligator purse.
When she screamed and jumped up, her alligator purse
got caught on Mrs. Rosebud's wig."

"But why did she jump up?"

"Because Miss Peachtree's poodle sneezed and sprayed cold punch on her back."

"That's impossible. How can a poodle sneeze punch?"

"I guess some got up his nose. You see, he was swimming in the punch bowl."

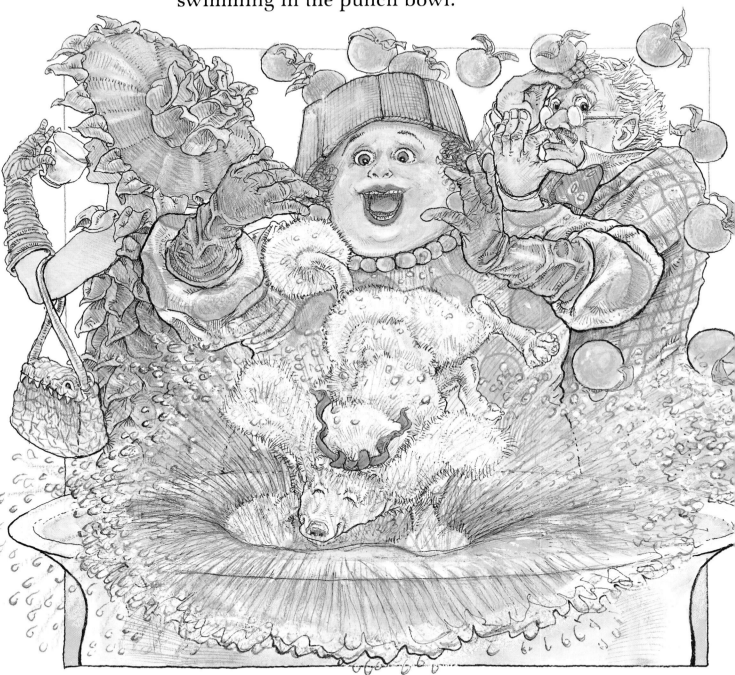

"You mean Miss Peachtree let her poodle dive into the punch bowl?"

"Actually, Miss Ivy hit her."

"What! The garden club ladies were socking punches
at each other?"

"No, Jimmy. They were sipping punch. But when Miss Ivy fainted, she hit Miss Peachtree, who dropped her poodle in the punch bowl. Nobody wanted any punch after that."

"But what made Miss Ivy faint?"

"Your boa constrictor."

"My boa? I thought he was asleep on your mom's head."

"Well, he sort of woke up when he smelled Miss Ivy's Yellow-Spotted Bongo plant."

"Her Yellow-Spotted what?"

"Well, Miss Ivy was giving a talk to the garden club about this rare Yellow-Spotted Bongo plant from South America. When she mentioned that its only natural enemy is the boa constrictor, well, your boa gobbled it up…pot and all."

"Oh, I see…so she fainted and hit Miss Peachtree, who dropped her poodle, who sneezed punch on Miss Greenleaf, whose alligator purse caught Mrs. Rosebud's wig."

"Yeah, and Mrs. Rosebud kept asking me to close the window because she felt a draft."

"But whatever happened to the poodle in the punch bowl,
   Meggie?"
"Oh, your boa ate it."

"The poodle?"

"No, Jimmy. He ate the punch bowl and saved the poodle!
The poodle was so grateful that he wouldn't leave
your boa's side."

"Wow! Can I serve cookies at your mom's next
garden club meeting?"

"I don't think so. She's not a member anymore."

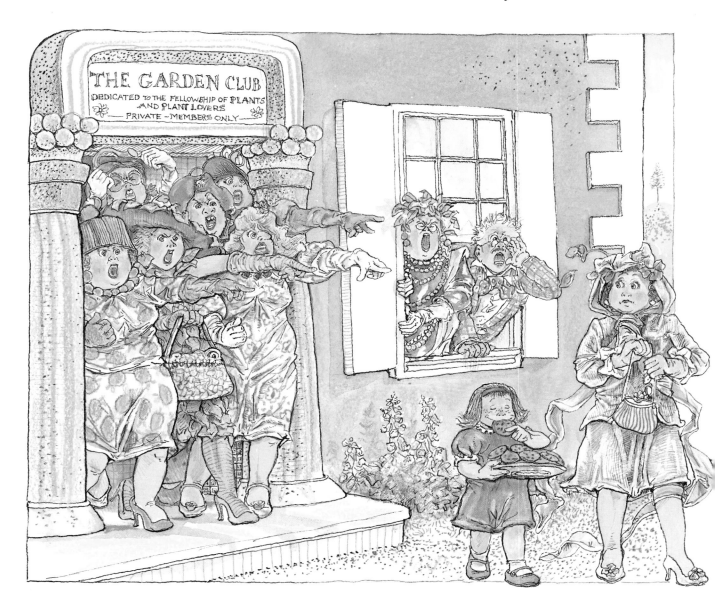

"Well, can we go back there and get my boa?"
"No, your boa left with Miss Peachtree's poodle.
Maybe they're at her house. Let's go see!"

The residence of
MISS OLGA PEACHTREE
AND HER POODLE

"Good, Peaches, you came home all by yourself."